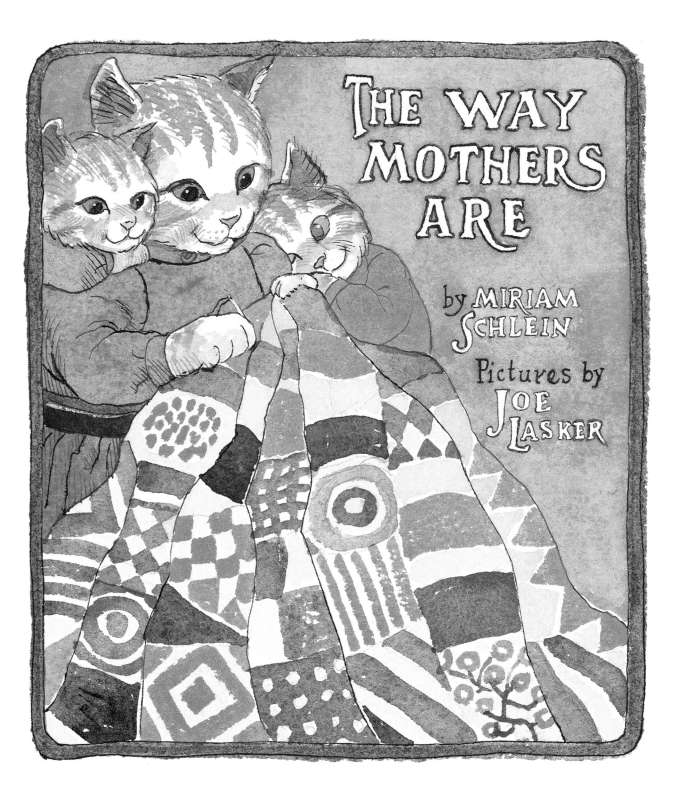

# THE WAY MOTHERS ARE

by MIRIAM SCHLEIN

Pictures by JOE LASKER

Albert Whitman & Company, Morton Grove, Illinois

The illustrations were done in pen
and indelible ink and transparent watercolor.
The text typeface is Bookman.

Text © 1963, 1991 by Miriam Schlein.
Illustrations © 1993 by Joe Lasker.
Published in 1963 by Albert Whitman & Company,
6340 Oakton Street, Morton Grove, Illinois 60053.
Second edition 1993.
Published simultaneously in Canada by
General Publishing, Limited, Toronto.
Printed in the United States of America.
10   9   8   7   6   5   4   3   2


Library of Congress Cataloging-in-Publication Data

Schlein, Miriam.
The way mothers are / Miriam Schlein;
illustrated by Joe Lasker.
—2nd ed.
p.   cm.
Summary: A little cat tries to figure out why his mother
loves him even when he is naughty, and if she loves him
at other times because he is good.
ISBN 0-8075-8691-9
[1. Mothers—Fiction. 2. Cats—Fiction.]
I. Lasker, Joe, I11. II. Title.
PZ7.S347Way  1993                        92-21516
[E]—dc20                                         CIP
                                                      AC

For Lee and Hy
and Caroline, too. J.L.

Mother," said the little one, swinging
on a tree, "do you love me?"
"Yes, I do," said the mother cat,
washing all the clothes.

"But Mother," said the little one, "*why* do you love me when sometimes I am naughty and run away when you are trying to dress me?"

"I never said I stopped loving you when you are naughty, did I?" asked his mother.

"No," said the little one, "you didn't.
But how can you love me when I scream
and SCREAM, the way you don't like?"

"I don't love you all the other time just because you are *not* screaming," said his mother. "So why should I stop loving you sometimes just because you *are* screaming?"

"I don't know," said the little one,
scratching his head.

"But Mother, how can you really love
me when sometimes I am naughty *all* day
long, when I grab things away from Sister,
and knock her down, and throw my
clothes all over the floor?"

"I can and do love you, even those days," said his mother. "Even though I don't really like one single thing you do."

"But why?" said the little one. "*Why* do you love me?"

"Why do you think?" asked his mother.

The little one thought for a minute and
said, "You love me because I am very
smart and can draw nice pictures!"

"You are smart, and you draw very nice
pictures. But that's not why I love you,"
said his mother.

The little one thought some more. Then
he said, "I know. You love me because
some days I am sweet to Sister and let her
play with my blocks, my wagon, all my
toys, and I push her gently on the swing!"

His mother said, "You make me happy
when you do all those nice things. But
that is not why I love you."

The little one thought and thought. Then he said, "I guess you love me then because so many days I eat what I should, and I brush my teeth and don't let the water splash all over the floor, and I sit very still in the car when we go someplace."

The little one took a deep breath.
"And, those days, I put my toys away, and
go to bed when I'm supposed to, too.
That's why you love me," he said—this
time very certain—"because lots of days I
am so good."

"It's awfully nice on those days when you are really so good," said his mother, sitting down at last. "But even that is not the reason I love you."

"Then why?" said the little one, and he took a flying leap and landed on his mother's lap. "Why *do* you love me?"

"I love you," she answered, "because you are *my* little one, my very own child. From the moment you were born, I cared for you, and wanted what was best for you.

"So you don't think I love you just when you're good, and stop loving you when you are naughty, do you? That's not the way mothers are. I love you all the time, because you are mine."

"Is that the reason?" asked the little one. "That's so simple!"

"Yes," said the mother, giving him a big, tight hug. "That's the reason. And it is so simple. But that's the way mothers are."

"I'm glad that's the way mothers are!" said the little one.

And he hugged her right back, very tight.